The Pumpkin and the Pantsuit

DEDICATED TO
EVERYONE WHO ISN'T
GIVING UP

A short, short time ago,
in a land not very far away, there lived
a Pumpkin and a Pantsuit.

The house wasn't just big,
it was beautiful.

Also, it came with an airplane,

a movie theater,

a room shaped like a circle,

a chef who made really good
mac n' cheese whenever you wanted it,

and a helicopter you
could park on the lawn.

Plus, if you live in the big white house, it means you're the boss of everyone!

There was just one problem.

Even though the house was huge, it only
had room for The Pumpkin *or* The Pantsuit.
Not both of them.

And it was up to all the people in the land
to decide which one it would be.

EVERYWHERE ELSE!

So The Pumpkin and The Pantsuit
thought long and hard.

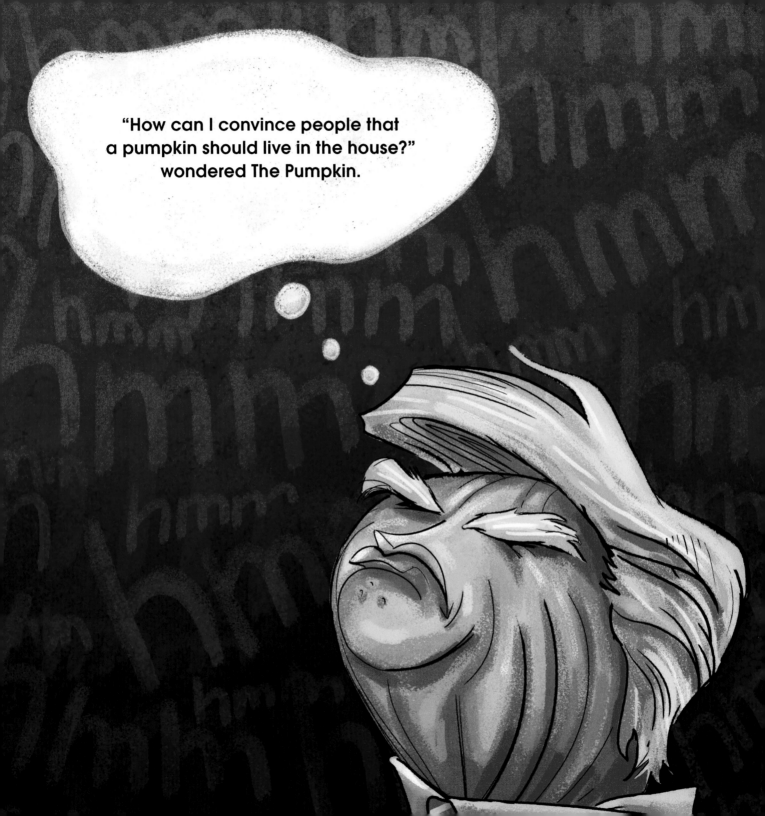

They decided to make speeches, lots of them.

They went on TV, pretty much every day.

They answered lots of questions, pointed and waved,
and gave the thumbs-up sign whenever they could.

They made sure their hair stayed in place
at all times, which for The Pumpkin required
a fair amount of effort.

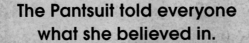

The Pantsuit told everyone
what she believed in.

The Pumpkin had a lot
of his own ideas.

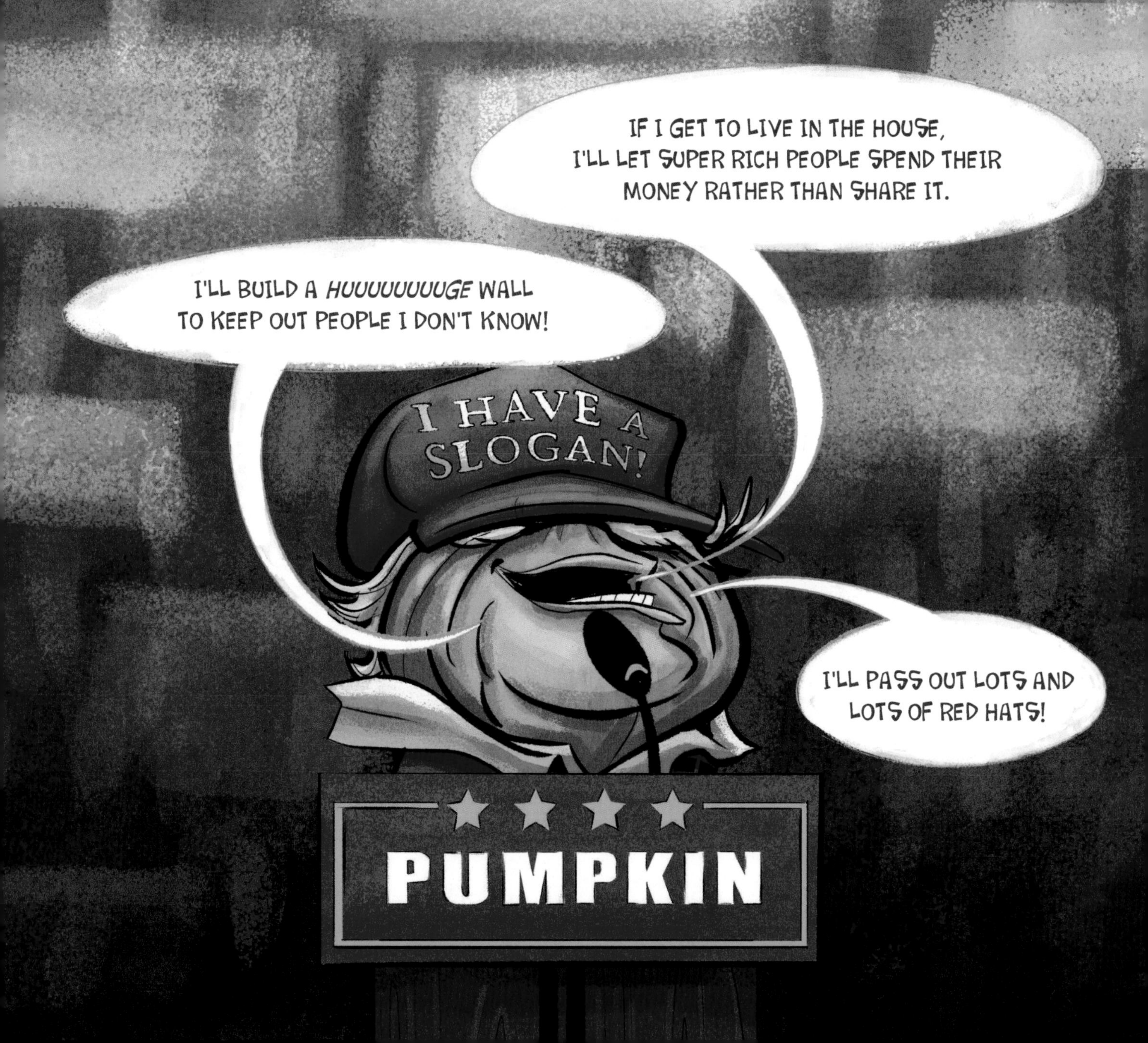

Of course,
no one is totally perfect.

Not The Pumpkin.

And not The Pantsuit either.

The Pumpkin made people upset too,
because The Pumpkin was a bully.

He said nasty things about people
he didn't even know.

He also said he could grab anything
he wanted just because he was famous.

Actually, there were lots of things
The Pumpkin did that people didn't like.

☑ b
☑ war
☑ creep
☑ say gro
☐ learn how
☑ blame China
☑ blame Pantsui
☑ blame media for
☑ blame Prez for stu
☑ send friend request
☑ discuss bringing back
☑ attack hispanic jud
☑ sniff
☑ suggest
☑ win

Finally,
the day came
to decide.

All across the land,
people went into places that
looked like shower stalls and
picked either The Pumpkin
or The Pantsuit.

A few people even picked some guy named Gary, mainly because they were tired of the whole thing.

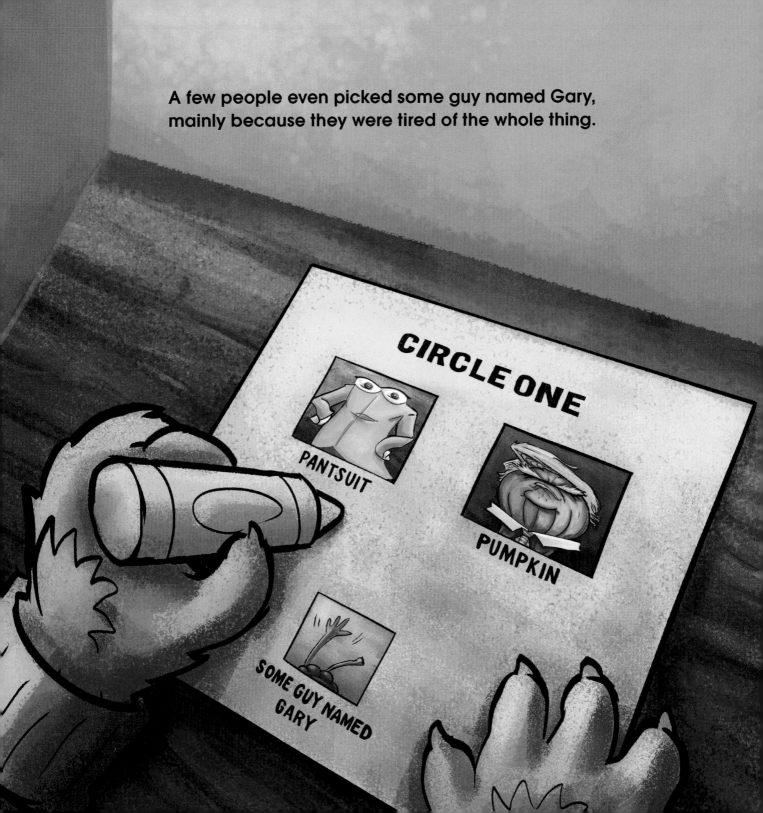

So.

Do you know
who won?

PUMPKIN WINS!
PUMPKIN WINS!
PUMPKIN TO LIVE IN BIG WHITE HOUSE

The Pumpkin did.

This made a lot of
people bummed out.

And bewildered.

And befuddled.

"How could this happen?" they asked.

After all, The Pumpkin was a bully.

And it didn't seem right that a bully was going to live in the big white house and be the boss of people.

He was already too bossy!

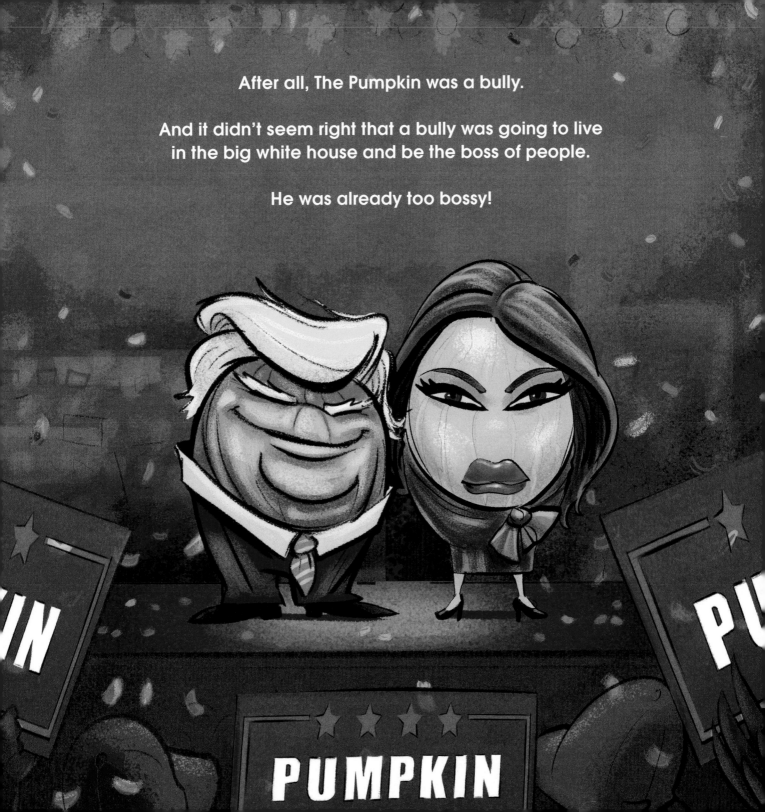

But The Pumpkin *was* going to live in the big white house.

And The Pantsuit wasn't.

Which, as you might expect,
made The Pantsuit feel sad.

So she did something that always helps
when you're feeling less than great.

She went outside
to walk her dog.

Then a funny thing happened,
in addition to her dog going pee.

All sorts of little pantsuits started running up to her.

Even though she didn't win, they were thanking her anyway!

Turns out, she had inspired the little pantsuits to believe that some day, very soon, one of *them* would live in the big white house!

Sure, maybe it wouldn't be today.
Or tomorrow. Or the day after that. Or even
two and a half weeks from now.

But some day,
it was *going* to happen!

This made The Pantsuit feel much less sad. She smiled a small smile, and went back to her house.

Not a big, white house, but a regular-sized brick house.

After all her hard work, The Pantsuit
needed a nice, long nap.

So she curled up on her
comfiest couch and closed
her sleepy eyes.

It wasn't long before
she was once again dreaming
big, shiny dreams.

not THE END

written by

TODD EISNER, JAMIE BARRETT
& PETE HARVEY

illustrated by

 the STUDIO

MIKE OCASIO, ALISON ABITBOL
& JUAN CARLOS MONT

Made in the USA
Middletown, DE
21 April 2017